Bobby Leach

Charles Stephens

lo
have in
a tortoise
Sunny Boy?

William "Red" Hill, Jr.

George Stathakis
&
Sunny Boy

Sunny Boy!

The Life and Times of a Tortoise

Candace Fleming
Pictures By
Anne Wilsdorf

Melanie Kroupa Books
Farrar, Straus and Giroux · New York

For the daredevil in all of us   —C.F.
For Julien and Alice   —A.W.

Distributed in Canada by Douglas & McIntyre Publishing Group
Color separations by Embassy Graphics
Printed and bound in the United States of America by Berryville Graphics
Designed by Barbara Grzeslo
First edition, 2005
1 3 5 7 9 10 8 6 4 2

www.fsgkidsbooks.com

Library of Congress Cataloging-in-Publication Data
Fleming, Candace.
    Sunny Boy!: the life and times of a tortoise / Candace Fleming ; pictures by
Anne Wilsdorf.— 1st ed.
        p.   cm.
    Summary: In this fictionalized account, Sunny Boy, a 100-year-old tortoise,
describes various events in his long life including the dangerous barrel ride over
Niagara Falls that he takes with his daredevil owner on July 5, 1930.
    ISBN-13: 978-0-374-37297-2
    ISBN-10: 0-374-37297-7
    1. Turtles—Juvenile fiction. [1. Turtles—Fiction.   2. Niagara Falls (N.Y.)—
Fiction.   3. Daredevils—Fiction.] I. Wilsdorf, Anne, ill.   II. Title.

PZ10.3.F624Su 2005
[E]—dc22

                                                                    2004040451

I have always longed for the quiet life.
Even as a hatchling, fresh from my egg, I never once frolicked or
played. No, I preferred slow-paced days and basking on sun-warmed rocks.

But one fateful morning, I was plucked from my rock like a grape from its vine.

Boxed . . . shipped . . . bound for the soup pots of New York City's finest restaurants!

But fate twists.

Instead of landing in hot water, I landed in Pelonius Pimplewhite's lap.

"What a fine-looking tortoise," said Pelonius.

And he took me home along with his leftover pork chops.

Pelonius, I soon learned, was a horticulturist—a grower of flowers. In his garden, he misted his lilies and sang to his orchids while I basked in the blossom-sweet sunlight.

One morning, as I rested in my usual bright spot, Pelonius
said, "You, my friend, are a very sunny boy."
I opened my eyes.
"Sunny Boy," he repeated. "It has a ring, doesn't it?"
It certainly did.
So Sunny Boy I was named.
And Sunny Boy I remained.
Year after quiet year.

But alas! Men do not live as long as tortoises. And one sad day, I went to live with his nephew . . .

CORNELIUS.

Dear, dear Cornelius!

I can still picture him—his magnifying glass pressed to his eye, his stamp tongs gripping his latest prize.

"Ah," he would gush. "Such color! Such design! Such postal marks!" And while I basked in a sunny spot atop a pile of stamp-collecting albums, we licked and stuck . . . licked and stuck . . .

Year after quiet year.

But woe! I outlived Cornelius, too. And so I went to live with his nephew . . .

Augustus.

What can I say about Augustus?
He was brilliant! A genius! A Latin scholar!

"*Veni, vidi, vici,*" he would intone while I basked in a sunny spot beside a bust of Caesar. "*E pluribus unum.*"

Year after quiet year.

But woe and alas! I outlived Augustus, too. And so I went to live with his nephew . . .

Biff!

WA-HOOO!

"I'm Biff the brave! Daredevil extraordinaire!"
D-d-daredevil?
My world tipped.

Now, instead of basking in the bright sunlight,
I bounced and jostled about in Biff's dank sidecar.
Instead of inhaling the sweet smell of orchids,
I choked on the fumes from his motorcycle as we roared
from one daredevil performance to the next.

And instead of the soothing sounds of stamp collecting and Latin verbs, my ears were filled with the boos of Biff's audiences.

Why boos, you ask.

Well . . .

In Buffalo, Biff the brave shot himself from a gigantic cannon.

He fizzled.

In Hoboken, he walked on the wings
of a high-flying biplane.
He flopped.

And in Toledo, he revved . . . roared . . . raced into a blazing ring of fire!

It took firemen three hours to put out the flames.

Poor Biff! Had I not been so utterly miserable, I might have felt sorry for him. Instead, I hoped he would learn from his failures and give up his daredevil dreams.

Sadly, the more Biff failed, the more determined he grew.

"All I need," he declared, "is one daring, dangerous, death-defying stunt. A stunt like . . . like . . .

"Niagara Falls!" he whooped. "I will go over Niagara Falls in a barrel. It will be the stunt of the century."

I shuddered in my shell.

But Biff packed up his gear.

Off we roared to Niagara Falls.

What a sight!

Above the furious falls raged a white-capped river.

Below boiled an angry stew of pounding water and jagged rock.

And in between?

A one-hundred-and-sixty-seven-foot drop!

I felt faint.

"Biff," I wanted to shout. "Don't do it! Don't do it!"

But his mind, I knew, was made up.

Unable to gaze upon those dangerous falls any longer, I crawled away and into . . .

Knott's Niagara Museum.
Instantly, the scent of orchids tickled my nose. I
followed the scent over . . . behind . . . and into the library.

A little girl was there—a little girl with an orchid in
her hair and a stamp-collecting book on her lap. Remarkably,
the book was written in—Latin!

"Hello," she said. "My name is Euphemia Knott. My
father is curator here. Would you like to hear something
interesting?" And she read, "*Veni, vidi, vici. E pluribus unum.*"

My heart swelled. Then . . .

"There you are!" hollered Biff. "Come on, Sunny Boy. We don't have time to poke around this joint. Tomorrow's the big day, and I still have a barrel to build." He grabbed me.

"Adieu, dear tortoise," Euphemia called. She blew me a kiss. "Farewell, sweet Sunny Boy."

I blinked back a tear. Farewell, Euphemia. May we meet again.

All that afternoon and late into the night, Biff
worked on his barrel.

He lined the inside with cushions for a softer ride.

He screwed a weight into the bottom so it would
float upright.

And he drilled three tiny air holes into the lid.

"So I can breathe," he explained.

While he worked, I worried about Biff . . .
dreamed of Euphemia . . . longed for the quiet life. In
that black moment, I even considered running away. But
tortoises do not run, and so I stayed, fretting and
fussing the dark hours away.

At first light, Biff rolled out the barrel.

Two rivermen awaited us. The first man grabbed the barrel. The second grabbed me.

"Listen, mister," said the first man. "This isn't the brightest idea. Those falls are dangerous."

"Yeah," added the second man. "Dangerous and deadly."

"Please, Biff," I begged with my eyes. "Listen to them."

Biff did not. Climbing into the barrel, he shouted, "On to the falls! To fame! To fortune!"

The first man had already put the lid on the barrel when the second man stopped him. "Hey! You forgot your tortoise," he called.

Tortoise?!

Quicker than Biff could shout, "Not Sunny Boy!" the barrel—and our fates—were sealed.

All I could do was burrow deep into my shell, and brace myself.

We rolled top over bottom. Bottom over top.
Sideways. Longways. Every which ways.

SLAM! BANG!
BOUNCE!

BOOM!

Then—how to explain it?—a sudden, unexpected sensation surged through me. For the first time in my long and quiet life, I felt exhilarated! Elated! Alive!

WA-HOOO!

Then . . .
Everything went black.

I awoke to the sound of Euphemia's voice.
"Sunny Boy," she exclaimed. "You're alive!"
Alive?
I shook my bruised and throbbing head.
Barely.

Later that afternoon, Biff made an announcement. "What I did today was stupid and dangerous," he said. "But I've learned my lesson. Never again will I risk life, limb, and friend for some dumb stunt. As of this moment, I'm giving up the daredevil life to become . . ."

My hopes soared. A horticulturist? A stamp collector? A Latin scholar?

"An explorer!" declared Biff. "I will climb Mount Everest. Row down the Congo River. Trek across the South Pole."

The South Pole?

I shivered.

"There's just one problem," added Biff. "As much as I enjoy your company, the South Pole's no place for a tortoise. So maybe . . ." He smiled at Euphemia. "Maybe . . . while I'm away . . . you could live with . . . her."

Euphemia?

Oh, joy!

Now I have orchids again. I have stamps. I have Latin.
Indeed, it is the quiet life.

And yet—dare I admit it?—sometimes the quiet life
is a bit *too* quiet.

That's when I look forward to Biff's visits. I look forward to those smelly fumes and that bouncy sidecar. Indeed, I look forward to going, for just a short time—fast!

WA-HOOO!

The Truth Behind the Tale

Since 1901, more than fifteen people have plunged over Niagara Falls in barrels or other odd contraptions—fifteen people and one tortoise.

This story is, of course, fiction, but it was inspired by a real-life tortoise named Sunny Boy. The real Sunny Boy was one hundred years old when he made the perilous trip. His owner was not a daredevil named Biff but rather a self-proclaimed writer and philosopher named George Stathakis. Much of Stathakis' writing didn't make sense, and his idea of philosophy included invented "conversations" with Plato and Socrates. Stathakis also claimed Sunny Boy could talk. "If I die, the tortoise will carry the secret of the trip, and reveal it at the proper time," Stathakis told reporters just before he and his tortoise climbed into their barrel.

Theirs was the biggest barrel to go over the falls. Made of four-inch-thick staves, held in place by strong steel hoops, the barrel's inside was padded with pillows to cushion the inevitable bouncing. It had a metal andiron screwed into the bottom to keep it floating upright and air holes drilled into its top to provide oxygen. Many people believed the tortoise and his owner had everything they needed to survive the journey.

On Saturday, July 5, 1930, at about 3:35 p.m., the red, white, and blue barrel containing reptile and man paused on the brink of the falls for a moment before it plummeted into the misty abyss. It did not come up.

As the day ended, the crowds dispersed. By 4:00 the next morning, even Stathakis' rescuers had given up hope. It wasn't until 1:30 p.m. on Sunday that the barrel was recovered from the lower river. It was damaged but intact. Inside, Sunny Boy was alive, but George Stathakis was not. He had suffocated from lack of oxygen.

Sunny Boy lived for another forty years at the Niagara Falls Museum. Allowed free rein, the tortoise crept through the marble hallways, basking in sunny spots, and chewing the lower leaves off the museum's rubber plant. He became a favorite of staff and visitors alike. But in all that time, Sunny Boy never revealed the secrets of his fateful trip.

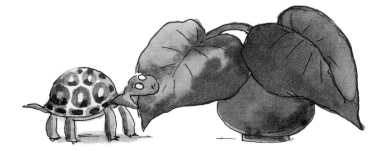

Jean Lussier 1928

William Fitzgerald
(alias Nathan Boya) 1961

They all

over Niagara

Steven Trotter
1985, 1995

Annie Taylor 1901